D0513588

Dick and Dom have reigned supreme for

many, many, many, many, many, many, many, many, many, many
many, many, many, many, many, many, many, many, many, many
many, many, many, many, many, many, many, many, many, many
many, many, many, many, many, many, many, many, many, many
many, many, many, many, many, many, many, many, many, many
many, many, many, many, many, many, many, many, many, many
many, many, many, many, many, many, many, many, many, many
many, many, many, many, many, many, many, many, many, many
many, many, many, many, many, many, many, many, many, many
many, many, many, many, many, many, many, many, many, many

years doing slightly naughty but very silly stuff
all over your telly box!

The End.

PS: Many!

# Dick and Dom's

SLIGHTLY **NAUGHTY**

BUT VERY **SILLY**

## WORDS

MACMILLAN CHILDREN'S BOOKS

FIRST PUBLISHED 2013 BY MACMILLAN CHILDREN'S BOOKS
A DIVISION OF MACMILLAN PUBLISHERS LIMITED
20 NEW WHARF ROAD, LONDON N1 9RR
BASINGSTOKE AND OXFORD
ASSOCIATED COMPANIES THROUGHOUT THE WORLD
WWW.PANMACMILLAN.COM

ISBN 978-1-4472-5639-7

TEXT AND ILLUSTRATIONS COPYRIGHT © RICHARD McCOURT AND DOMINIC WOOD 2013
ILLUSTRATED AND CO-WRITTEN BY DAVE CHAPMAN

THE RIGHT OF RICHARD McCOURT AND DOMINIC WOOD TO BE IDENTIFIED AS
THE AUTHORS OF THIS WORK HAS BEEN ASSERTED BY THEM IN
ACCORDANCE WITH THE COPYRIGHT, DESIGNS AND PATENTS ACT 1988.

1 3 5 7 9 8 6 4 2

A CIP CATALOGUE RECORD FOR THIS BOOK IS AVAILABLE FROM
THE BRITISH LIBRARY.

PRINTED AND BOUND BY CPI GROUP (UK) LTD, CROYDON CR0 4YY

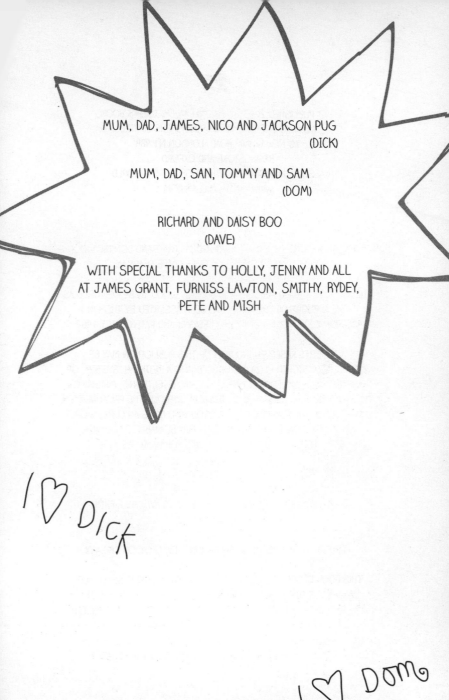

MUM, DAD, JAMES, NICO AND JACKSON PUG
(DICK)

MUM, DAD, SAN, TOMMY AND SAM
(DOM)

RICHARD AND DAISY BOO
(DAVE)

WITH SPECIAL THANKS TO HOLLY, JENNY AND ALL
AT JAMES GRANT, FURNISS LAWTON, SMITHY, RYDEY,
PETE AND MISH

I ♡ DICK

I ♡ DOM

PARENTAL GUIDANCE NOTICE...

Hello, Parents, it's me, Pretend David Bowie - Just here as a Guardian of good taste. This is a lovely little read. Ziggggy.

# CONTENTS

# INTRODUCTION

It was with a pen and paper that over the years Dick and Dom wrote this book for you, yes, you – sitting there with duck egg on your chin. A book that is a dictionary of wrongness, a file of fanamawabbles*, and most importantly a book that brings you slightly naughty but very silly words that are perfectly OK to say in front of adults of all varieties, shapes and sizes.

If your homework is late and the teacher asks you what happened, simply smile charmingly at them and say, 'FWATS' (page 43), or if your mum or dad asks you why you haven't eaten your veg, just shout out 'I'm A BIG BABBA-BUBBA BLIMP' (page 7). Get cheeky, without getting told off!

So read, learn and regurgitate these genius words in your home, school or oil rig, and you TOO can be as slightly naughty but very silly as Dick and Dom.

Now turn the page, you lazy lunk, and get started!

*Incredibly brilliant nonsense

1

# DOBBAWOOFS . . . INNIT

A person who has just
trumped and blamed the dog

# MUSTY TROUTWARBLER

An aged teacher who can't keep
control of the class

# GREEN FAIRY ROPE

Stringy bogies

# GERM RAIN

The little bits of spit that some
teachers do when they're talking

# BIG BABBA-BUBBA BLIMP

A baby who exists only on junk food

## LONG BONGOS

### Runny snot

# BADBUMS DA VINCI

The mark on your pants when your
bum has done bad art

# DUMP-ASAURUS

A poo big enough to have come
from a dinosaur

# CO-JOINED WEASLEY

A geeky person who is best friends
with a cool person to try and make
themselves seem cooler

# SECONDHAND PUS LILO

 A used plaster floating in
the swimming pool

## JUMBO CHICKEN WINGS

The bit of skin on your nan's
elbow that you can stretch

# MCBOOSH-DOOSH

A sneeze that showers your
friends with sneeze juice

# COBBLER WOBBLER

A person who makes crazy statements
that could never be true

## UMBABBA

A large auntie who always has sweets

# UMBUTU

A small auntie who gives you money

UMBOBO

A normal-sized auntie who
hasn't got any sweets

# UMBACCA

An auntie who looks like
they may be related to an
intergalactic hairy monster

# COLONEL PATATASWAT

A very sweaty friend who
smells like Marmite

# DITZY VORDERMAN

The moment you realize you
can't solve a maths question

# FLOBBORAFT

A small (or large) amount of someone
else's flob floating in the sea – that almost
magnetically keeps coming your way

# BIG DOG

A surprisingly loud burp ◌

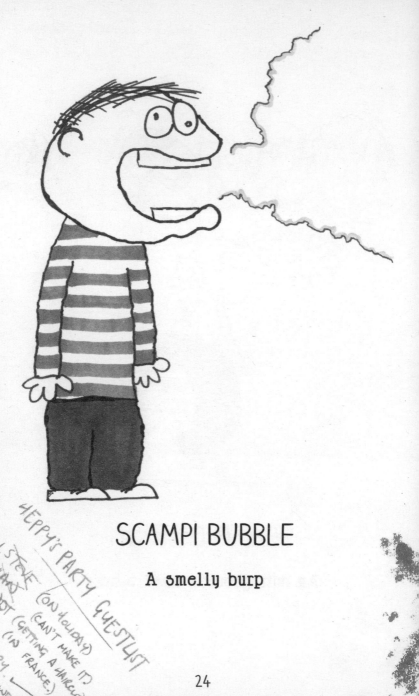

# SCAMPI BUBBLE

### A smelly burp

# SCAMPI CANNON

An outrageously smelly burp

## KREFT

A dusty sweet from your nan's handbag

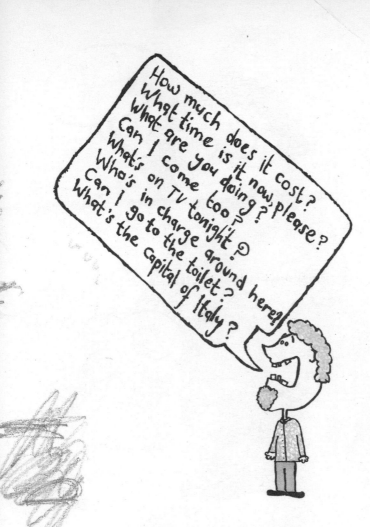

# LITTLE NOELLY

A short person who asks far
too many questions

# BOMB ROTTER

A trump so loud and stinky that it
makes people instantly jump off their
chairs, run out of doors and generally
evacuate the area at incredibly high
speed as if in a disgusting stunt show

# POSH BILLY-BAGPIPES

Somebody who talks all posh – but
only when they're trying to be clever
or when there are other poshies about

# BOBBY'S BITS

The selection of dust and hair that
lies in the corners of all carpets
which is placed there by Bobby the
fairy dustman and his mate Dave

30

# TWAGGLEBORKS

British teenagers who watch so
much American TV that their brains
think they're actually American, and
say lots of American-ish things

# HOPPER-VON-FROGGY WHOPPER

A DVD that gets shifted from the DVD player on to the side, then from case to case, but never makes it home to its original case

# FROODLES

The red lines around the bottom of
your legs that your socks leave behind
to remind you of them

# BOO-BOO MELON

An embarrassing baby photo of you with
googly eyes and a head shaped like a melon
that your parents have on the wall

# OSWALDCHOPS

The inability to drink properly after a
dentist has used anaesthetic on your mouth
– usually involving large-scale dribbling

# FUTTOCS

The feeling that you get just as you realize you've trodden barefoot on a hairbrush, a piece of Lego, some keys or an upturned plug

# BURTON FUTTOCS

The fall to the floor clutching
your foot that directly follows
an attack of futtocs

37

OLLY MARS.

# FUTTOC FEATURES

The screwed-up face you make as you
rub your foot after a burton futtocs

# DR FUTTOCS

The act of rubbing your foot really quickly in a hopeless attempt to cure the pain of the futtocs

# GANGAMOO

A noisy bunch of people all talking too
loudly to each other about themselves

# FILTHY IGLOO

When you trump under the duvet
and it amplifies the power of
the trump's smellification

## YAK YAK TRUMPET

Unexpected sick

# FWATS

Hair lice

# SLEEPY ELVIS

When you have just woken up
and become a morning mumbler

## WHISPERING TO RALPH

When you're being sick but no sick is coming up, so you end up making a frequent whispering sound which sounds like the boy's name 'Ralph', as if you're trying to wake up an invisible Ralph

# DINING WITH GENERAL SEWERS

Someone with outrageously smelly breath.
For example: 'What a stink, he must have
been dining with General Sewers!'

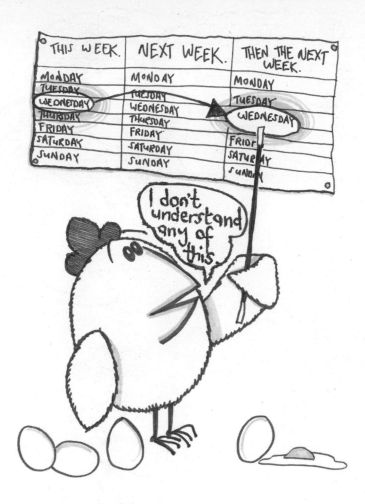

# WEDNESDAY FORTNIGHT

The amount of time exactly two weeks
from this coming Wednesday

## TWO-TONE TONY

When you do a poo that's soooooo big
it's half in and half out of the water –
giving it two different colours

48

# SAHARAHOOTA

Dry bogies

# PARSON'S GREEN

The contents of an old
man's handkerchief

## WARM WINNIE

Bellybutton fluff, also known as 'an Ant's Duvet'

# SACKANACKER

A ridiculously overactive toddler

# GEOFFREY BABBLES

A friend of your family who doesn't do or say anything interesting and instead just stands about looking awkward and asking silly questions

## BUM ALARM

The feeling you get just
before you need a poo

Mr and Mrs Plop.

Plip.

# PLIP

A very small plop

# HALF A HAIRY CHINNY-VON-MARY

A teenage boy who is unsuccessfully
growing facial hair

# UNI-GUMMIDGE

Someone with a large
percentage of gum in their smile
who rides a unicycle

# FIDGEWOCK

A disgusting swearword
never to be used

# ANTI-PAXMAN

The completely unconnected response
you give to a barrage of questions
you don't want to answer

# PRE-DINGLES

When you accidentally sing just before
everyone else does and they all stare
at you like you've dropped one

## STILTON TROTTER

A friend with very smelly feet

Hi, Y'all. My nose is full of dirty salt jelly.

But if you don't like my organic stuff why not make some DSJ® of your own?...

INGREDIENTS:

Dirt  Salt  Jelly

METHOD: MIX 'EM.

# DIRTY SALT JELLY

Wet and slightly bouncy bogies

62

# QUANGO DADDY

A dad who thinks he is the World's Best
Dancer but is actually terrible at dancing

# SMUGTROUGH

A person who has a far superior
lunchbox selection to you

# SHERBET MUGGINS

Someone who always looks terribly
pleased with themselves

# FAGIN DIRTBUCKET

A boy or girl whose face always appears
unclean, even after it's been washed

# GOZ WASH

When an adult produces a tissue, spits on it and then uses it to somehow 'wash' their son or daughter's face

# HAM HERMIT

A very small snorting pig. People who have ham hermits living in their noses appear to snort when they laugh. It is, in fact, the ham hermits snorting as they are humourless and laughter angers them

# ULLY MULLY

The teeny bits of food that somehow
escape your mouth and swim around your
water bottle like plankton on holiday

# QUON

The bits of old toothpaste juice and food
that sometimes hide in your toothbrush

# SCHNOZ BOOBLAY

The instantly inflated balloon of
snot that occurs when snotty-nosed
people laugh too hard

Hair from Bath plug

A Rat

Rat-a-toupée

# RATATOUPÉE

The hair you find in the bath or shower plughole, often recycled by dandy rats as a 'fancy' wig

# VOM GOBLIN

A burp with a small surprise
serving of sick

73

# CRUNCHY NUT EYE-NUTS

The small bits of stuff that you find in
the corner of your eyes in the morning,
also known as 'Spider's Cornflakes'

# OAPY WRINK-LOADS

Old folk in love

OLDEN DAYS MUSIC FILE.
Drag needle over this bit
to get music. (no, really.)

# NESBIT BURNS

The resulting injury of a knee slide,
elbow scrape or wall scratch

# POISON CUSTARDS

Small portions of yellow pus that seep
from the scabs caused by Nesbit Burns

# WAFFLING WAH-WAHS

Men you see on the TV news or politics shows who just gabble on about uninteresting nonsense

# CRUDDLE

General deposits people have been
kind enough to leave on the floor of the
changing room at the swimming pool

# WOT DAT

Something in your meal that should not be there and makes you say, 'Wot dat?'

# POTTY SWIPE

Toilet roll

# HOW TO USE SLIGHTLY NAUGHTY BUT VERY SILLY WORDS

Once upon a time Dick was in a sweet shop with five pounds given to him by his UMBUTU because his UMBOBO (who was slightly UMBACCA) refused to give him any sweets other than a KREFT.

Dom arrived, being a LITTLE NOELLY with really bad COLONEL PATATASWAT.

DOM

Hello! Can I have some of your sweets? Cos my BIG BABBA-BUBBA BLIMP has eaten all mine.

Along came their other friend Dave who was a POSH BILLY-BAGPIPES. Together they looked like a right group of TWAGGLEBORKS.

The sweet-shop owner arrived back from the dentist with a severe case of OSWALDCHOPS. 'Sorry I'm late, lads,' he dribbled, 'but I started my day with a FILTHY IGLOO which made me YAK YAK TRUMPET.'

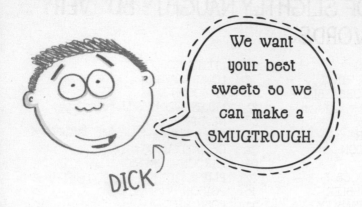

We want your best sweets so we can make a SMUGTROUGH.

DICK

'It will have to wait!' drooled the shopkeeper, grabbing his JUMBO CHICKEN WINGS. 'My BUM ALARM has just gone off and I don't want to do a BADBUMS DA VINCI!'

With that he did a MCBOOSH-DOOSH all over their faces, started doing a QUANGO DADDY and yelled, 'I'll see you WEDNESDAY FORTNIGHT.'

IF YOU WANT TO SHARE YOUR OWN **SLIGHTLY NAUGHTY BUT VERY SILLY WORDS** GO TO WWW.GOBSTOPPERBOOKS.COM

# INDEX OF SLIGHTLY NAUGHTY BUT VERY SILLY WORDS

# BONUS RUBBISH.

HEY, LOOK AT THAT!

WOW, IT REALLY IS RUBBISH.

FREE 'CUT-OUT AND KEEP' STUFF

'PAPER BUTTON' USELESS.

'REALISTIC' GARDEN PEA TO AMUSE AND FOOL YOUR FAMILY.

FREE → HALLOWEEN PUMPKIN BADGE! (GREAT FUN IF YOUR NAME'S TREVOR.)

TREVOR

FREE MAP OF SHROPSHIRE

FREE SILHOUETTE OF AN ANGRY CROW →

FREE BUS RIDE AROUND TOWN WITH 12 VOUCHERS

INCREDIBLE!

BUS RIDE VOUCHER 1

# FREE

'Paper Effect' Mirror frame...

BUY A MIRROR AND GLUE IT INTO THIS FREE GIFT FRAME. YOURS TO CUT OUT AND KEEP FOREVER.

Awesome.

# FREE

'Family Photo' It's Tommy, Sammy Daisy, Richard and Jackson the dog.

IN NEXT WEEK'S ISSUE →
(Even though this isn't a comic and there is no issue next week.)

# FREE

HOUSE IN NOTTINGHAM

AND a lifetime's supply of cat food. MIAOW

WHAT ARE YOU
LOOKING HERE FOR?
THE BOOK HAS
ENDED.


SHOVE OFF!